AUTHOR'S NOTE

Each of the Gospel writers tells the story of the Palm Sunday procession, when Jesus rides into Jerusalem on a colt while the people sing, cheer, and wave palm branches in the air. This procession was meant to mirror King Solomon's triumphal entry into Jerusalem and to fulfill the prophesies of the Old Testament. Although Israel had been conquered by the Romans, the Jewish people believed that God would send a king to set them free from their oppressors. Some thought this king would ride into Jerusalem on a war horse, with soldiers and swords, wearing a crown. But many looked for a king of peace, as described by Zechariah in Chapter 9, verse 9: "See, your king comes to you, gentle and riding on a colt, the foal of a donkey." Jesus and his disciples were saying: "This is it. It's happening *now,* just as the prophets promised. This is the king we've been waiting for, and he will be a king of peace."

People waved palm branches because of Old Testament prophesies and the stories of Solomon's royal procession. The palm was thought to be sacred, the "tree of life." It was carved on the walls and doors of Solomon's temple and was a symbol connecting Jesus with the glorious kings of Israel's past. On Palm Sunday today, people still march in processions and wave palm branches, remembering this event in the life of Jesus. But what does a young donkey know of towns and crowns and kings? Our little colt knows his hillside, but most of all, he knows about peace.

MARNI MCGEE

THE COLT AND THE KING

by Marni McGee

illustrated by John Winch

HOLIDAY HOUSE / New York

I, said the donkey, am old,

but still I remember a day long ago

when I was just a colt.

Spring had come to my hillside—

the time when lilies bloom

and sheep give birth to their lambs.

My owner took me away that day,

down to the village gate.

We waited there till strangers came:

men who said they needed a colt,

one that had never been ridden.

My owner sent me with them!

I pulled hard against my rope,

but the strangers' hands were strong.

I had to follow where they led.

We walked through the twisting streets,

where shouts and the rumble of wagons

drowned out the sound of the doves

and robbed the wind of its song.

We came at last to a place

where olives grew.

A noisy crowd had gathered there.

They swarmed like bees on ripened figs.

I bared my teeth.

My gray coat twitched.

My neck grew tight with fear.

In the midst of it all stood a man.

The strangers called him Jesus,

but many called him King.

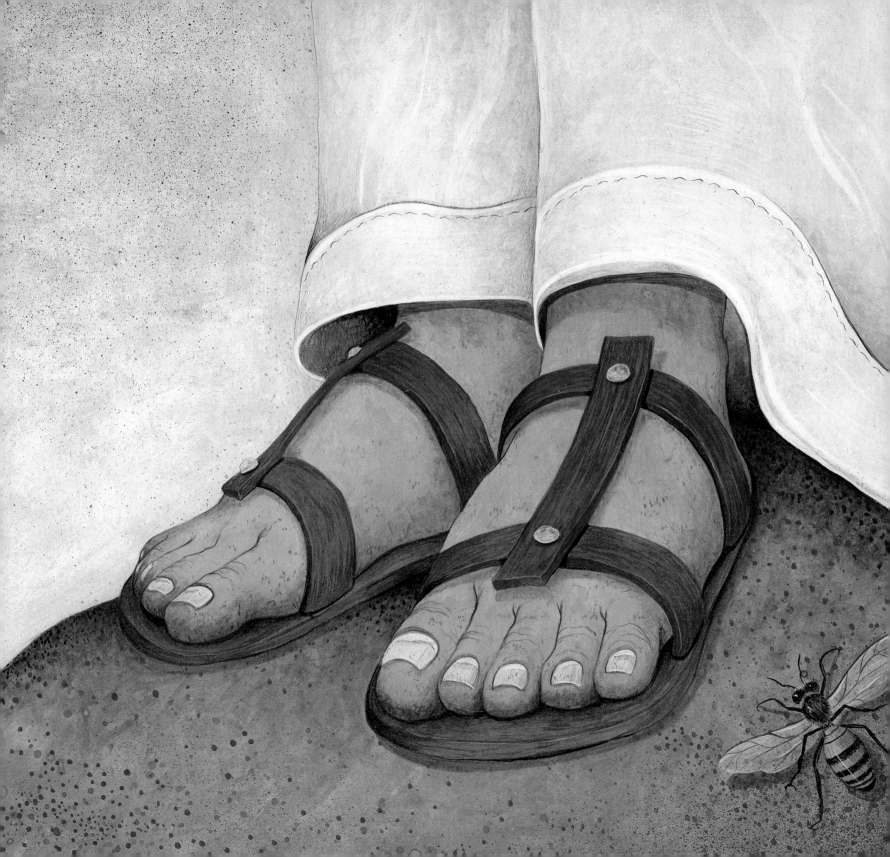

Jesus saw me tremble.

He came and stood beside me,

his hand upon my back.

In his voice was a river of quiet;

in his touch, a shelter of peace.

And my fear flew away

like a bird set free.

The people cut branches of palm

and waved them in the air.

They tossed their cloaks upon the path.

Then they lifted Jesus up

to set him on my back.

They danced and sang as we walked:

"Blessed is he who comes to save us.

Blessed is he who rides

triumphant on a colt."

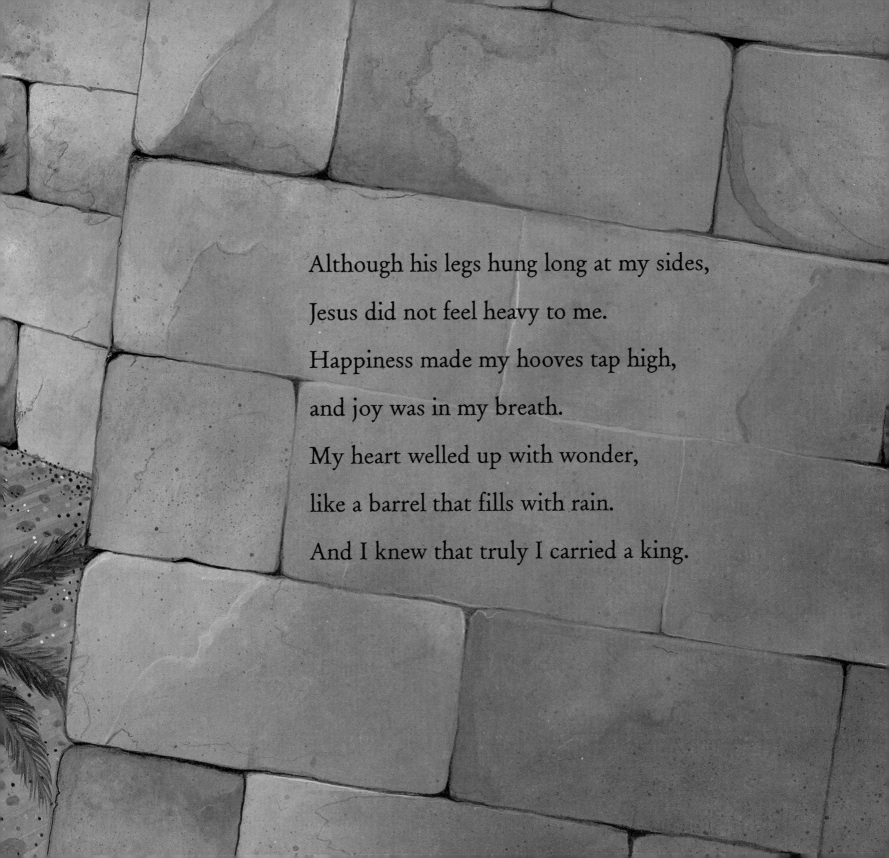

Although his legs hung long at my sides,

Jesus did not feel heavy to me.

Happiness made my hooves tap high,

and joy was in my breath.

My heart welled up with wonder,

like a barrel that fills with rain.

And I knew that truly I carried a king.

Yet how I longed to take him away,
far from that worrisome crowd!

I longed to take him home to my hillside.

There I would share my friends with him:

the mooing cow, the chuckling hen,

the lizard, the cricket, the crow.

I have not seen Jesus since that day.

But still, even now, my long ears prick,

listening for his voice.

I know that someday he will come,

and I will share my straw with him.

I will soften it with my hooves,

so he can lie down to rest.

My hillside will be a throne for him,

and at night the stars will weave him a crown.

In loving memory of my uncle,
Thomas Benton Sellers, Jr.,
and in honor of my brother,
Claude U. Broach, Jr.
M. M.

For Ben & Amalia
J. W.

Text copyright © 2002 by Marni McGee
Illustrations copyright © 2002 by John Winch
All Rights Reserved
Printed in the United States of America
The text typeface is Old Claude.
The artwork was created with impasto acrylic
on handmade French watercolor paper.
www.holidayhouse.com
First Edition

Library of Congress Cataloging-in-Publication Data
McGee, Marni.
The colt and the king / by Marni McGee; illustrated by John Winch.—1st ed.
p. cm.
Summary: A donkey tells how he reluctantly played a part in Jesus' entry
into Jerusalem on the first Palm Sunday.
ISBN 0-8234-1695-X (hardcover)
[1. Donkeys—Fiction. 2. Jesus Christ—Entry into Jerusalem—Fiction.
3. Palm Sunday—Fiction.] I. Winch, John, 1944– ill. II. Title.

PZ7.M167515 Co 2002
[E]—dc21
2001039235

BFT
5/04
16.95